From his home on the other side of the moon, Father Time summoned eight of his most trusted storytellers to bring a message of hope to all children. Their mission was to spread magical tales throughout the world: tales that remind us that we all belong to one family, one world; that our hearts speak the same language, no matter where we live or how different we look or sound; and that we each have the right to be loved, to be nurtured, and to reach for a dream.

This is one of their stories.
Listen with your heart and share the magic.

For Sylvie and
her uncle Rick,
whose capacity
to love has
awakened our
hearts.

Our thanks to artists Shanna Grotenhuis, Jane Portaluppi, and Mindi Sarko,
as well as Sharon Beckett, Yoshie Brady, Andrea Cascardi, Solveig Chandler, Jun Deguchi,
Akiko Eguchi, Liz Gordon, Tetsuo Ishida, William Levy, Michael Lynton, Masaru Nakamura,
Steve Ouimet, Tomoko Sato, Isamu Senda, Minoru Shibuya, Jan Smith, and Hideaki Suda.

THE LITTLE SNOW BEAR
An Original American Tale

Elizabeth
Rimassa

Flavia Weedn & Lisa Weedn Gilbert

Illustrated by Flavia Weedn

Hyperion • New York

Once upon a time, in a village near a great forest, there lived a little bear.

Although there were other bears who lived nearby in the village, they were all much older and much bigger.

No matter how hard he tried, he could never run as fast or jump as high as they could. And no matter how much he pretended to be as big as they were, he was still just a little bear.

Because of this the little bear was very sad and lonely, and more than anything he wished for a friend to be with—someone just like him.

One winter day he saw the other bears playing in the snow. They were making snowpeople. The little bear knew he couldn't make snowpeople as big as the others could. But maybe he could make a little bear out of snow—a little bear just like him—and maybe this little snow bear could be his friend.

So late that night, in his backyard where no one could see him, he began.

The little bear worked and worked, and by early morning he was finished. He had made a wonderful snow bear that looked just like him. At last he had a friend of his very own.

The little bear gave his friend a coat, a scarf, and boots, and they played together in the snow all day until it got dark.

"Remember now," said the snow bear to the little bear, "I am made out of snow, so I must sleep outside in the cold."

The little bear understood this and was so happy to have a friend that he made a bed for the snow bear just outside his own bedroom window.

All through the night, whenever the little bear
would awake, he would peek through the window to
see the snow bear. He was afraid it was all a dream,
but it wasn't, for the snow bear was always there.

Every day the two little friends would play together. Sometimes they would read books to each other, play games in the snow, or fly the little bear's kite.

And every night the little bear would go inside his house to sleep while the snow bear would sleep just outside his window.

What they liked to do best was to lie outside on the little bear's favorite quilt and look up at the night sky. They would watch the stars and the moon, and they would wonder about the world.

It was the best winter the little bear had ever known, and he never felt lonely, not even once. He was so very, very happy.

Then one night the snow bear
had something important to tell
the little bear. "Tomorrow," he
said, "is the first day of spring,
so I will have to go away. I am
made of snow, so I must follow
the winter and the frost."

The little bear cried and cried
and said, "Oh, please don't leave
me. You are my best friend, my
only friend."

The snow bear took the little
bear's hand and answered softly,
"But I will come back when the
winter comes again, and we will
play together just like we do
now, I promise."

The next morning the little bear looked out the window and saw that the snow bear had melted away. There beside the bed the little bear had made for him were the snow bear's scarf, coat, and boots—but the snow bear was gone.

Then the little bear noticed that something was inside one of the boots. It was a note from the snow bear.

It read: "It is true, I am your friend, but I am not your only friend. After I have gone, you will realize you have other friends, and you will discover a brand-new friend— a friend called 'remembering.'"

The little bear was still sad, but all through that day and the next few days he kept thinking about the snow bear and how much he missed him. Then he began to think about all the wonderful things they had done together.

He remembered how they had read books and pretended and how they had tried to sing songs with the snowbirds. He remembered how they had laughed when they had flown his kite and how they had watched the moon and stars in the night sky and how they had shared the wonder of the world together.

In his heart he remembered everything. Then he
began to realize he still had all these things. The
snowbirds were still there. They were his friends. His
kite was still there, and it was his friend. And the
moon and stars, they were his friends, too. They were
still up in the sky just like they had been before.

The snow bear had been right—the little bear did have other friends. And now the little bear understood what the snow bear's note meant about discovering that "remembering" was a friend, too.

By remembering the snow bear, the little bear was keeping his friend close to him. It was almost like doing all the things they had done together all over again—and this made the little bear feel good inside.

All through the year the little bear could hardly wait for the winter to come again so that he could tell the snow bear the wonderful things he had discovered about friendship and the magic of remembering.

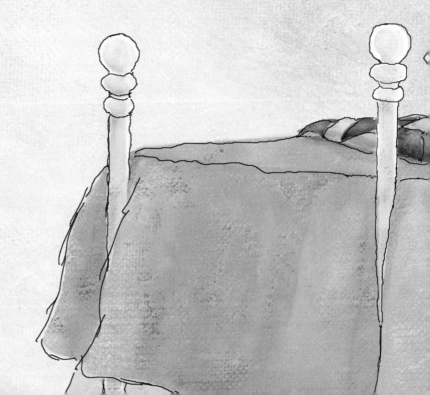

And then, finally, the winter came and with it came the little snow bear, just as he had promised. And for every winter after that, the two little friends were always together.

The little bear was never lonely again, for he was too busy making memories, memories he would keep forever, with his special friend made out of snow.

Produced in cooperation with Dream Maker Studios AG.
Printed in Singapore.
For information address Hyperion Books for Children,
114 Fifth Avenue, New York, New York 10011.

FIRST EDITION
1 3 5 7 9 10 8 6 4 2

Library of Congress Cataloging-in-Publication Data

Weedn, Flavia.
The little snow bear: an original American tale/written by
Flavia Weedn & Lisa Weedn Gilbert; illustrated by Flavia Weedn.
p. cm.—(Dream maker stories)
Summary: A snow bear comes to life and befriends a lonely little bear.
ISBN 0-7868-0044-5
[1. Bears—Fiction. 2. Friendship—Fiction. 3. Snow—Fiction] I. Gilbert, Lisa Weedn.
II. Title. III. Series: Weedn, Flavia. Dream maker stories.
PZ7.W4145Li 1995
[E]—dc20   94–11278   CIP AC

The artwork for each picture is digitally mastered using acrylic on canvas.
This book is set in 17-point Bernhard Modern.